THE QUICKEST KID IN CLARKSVILLE

BY
PAT ZIETLOW
MILLER

ILLUSTRATED BY
FRANK
MORRISON

chronicle books · san francisco

I'm running in place,
listening to my feet pound the pavement.

Pretending I'm the fastest woman in the world.

Of course, Wilma Rudolph—who grew up right in this
town—is faster than anyone. But I'm the quickest
kid in Clarksville, Tennessee.

And everyone around here knows it.

I'm thinking about tomorrow's parade and wondering what Wilma's three Olympic gold medals would feel like hanging 'round my neck, when a girl I've never seen before comes sashaying my way like she owns the sidewalk and everything on it.

She sticks a hand on her hip. "I'm Charmaine."
I look her up and down. "I'm Alta. That's Dee-Dee and Little Mo."
"Got me some new shoes," Charmaine says.

Boy-howdy, does she ever. Brand-new, only-been-worn-by-her shoes with stripes down the sides and laces so white they glow.

Shoes to *strut* in. Shoes to *run* in.

Because Charmaine's strutting hard enough to shame a rooster.

And her legs are just raring to run.

"These shoes are like Wilma's," she says. "My daddy went uptown to get 'em."

I stare at the concrete. I don't have a shoe-buying daddy. My sneakers have holes in the soles and laces that never thought to glimmer.

I bite my lip. It's OK.
Wilma wore a leg brace and flour-sack
dresses before she got big.

"Shoes don't make you fast," I say.
Charmaine's face tightens.

"Reckon I'm faster than *anyone*."
I puff up like a spitting cat. She wishes she were Wilma.
But I'm the real deal.
I point to the mailbox. "There and back."

We crouch low. Dee-Dee and Little Mo
count down, and we're off.
My sneakers slap a sidewalk beat.
Wil-ma Ru-dolph. Wil-ma Ru-dolph.

I reach the box first, turn and sprint back.
Arms moving. Legs grooving.
I hear Charmaine huffing and puffing.

Behind me.

I do a victory dance while Charmaine glares.
I'm still be-bopping when she takes off again.
"To the corner," Charmaine calls over her shoulder.
"Starting now."

I leap after her like a scalded frog. Wilma's come
from behind to win some of her races.
And so will I.
Wil-ma Ru-dolph. Wil-ma Ru-dolph.

When Charmaine reaches the corner, I'm nipping her ankles.

Bodies lunge. Feet tangle.

I fall. Charmaine stays up. And wins.
OUCH! My toe hurts. Probably 'cause it's poking out a brand-new hole.

Just like that, I puff up again.
"You tripped me! I would've
won if you didn't."
"You were in my lane. I won
fair and square."

Charmaine walks away, shaking her
braids and swinging her bottom. I
follow, mad as any cat. That's when
it happens. My toe hits a rock.
That rock hits Charmaine.

For a minute, Charmaine looks
like she might fight. But she leaves
without a word.

I limp home. Feet dragging. Head hanging.

I show Mama the hole. She sighs.
"Oh, baby girl. Those shoes have to last."

When parade day dawns,
I'm making a banner with Dee-Dee and
Little Mo. Then, Charmaine struts by
like she's queen of the block.

I scowl at her. Then I pick up the banner
and nod to Dee-Dee and Little Mo.

"Let's go."

Thing is, that banner is bulky. No way I'll make
it all the way to the parade.

It might be easier if I run. I force my feet to move.
But one block in, I can't go on.
I hear the beat of feet.

Wil-ma Ru-dolph.
Wil-ma Ru-dolph.

Charmaine is running by me. "Pass that here," she says.
I clutch the banner tighter. I don't need her help.
"Come on," says Charmaine. "We'll do it like Wilma's relay.
Three people ran it with her, you know."

I hate to admit it, but she's right.

I hand her the banner, and she takes off for
the next block. Then Dee-Dee takes a turn
and even Little Mo.

We run faster and faster, till our legs are nothing but a whirling blur. Just like you-know-who's.

People stare. Eyes popping. Fingers pointing. "You go, girls!" someone calls.

I sneak a look at Charmaine.
Her feet are flying.
Who's faster? I can't tell.
But Charmaine isn't strutting.
Or scowling.
She looks happy.
I don't mean to, but I smile.
Charmaine smiles back.

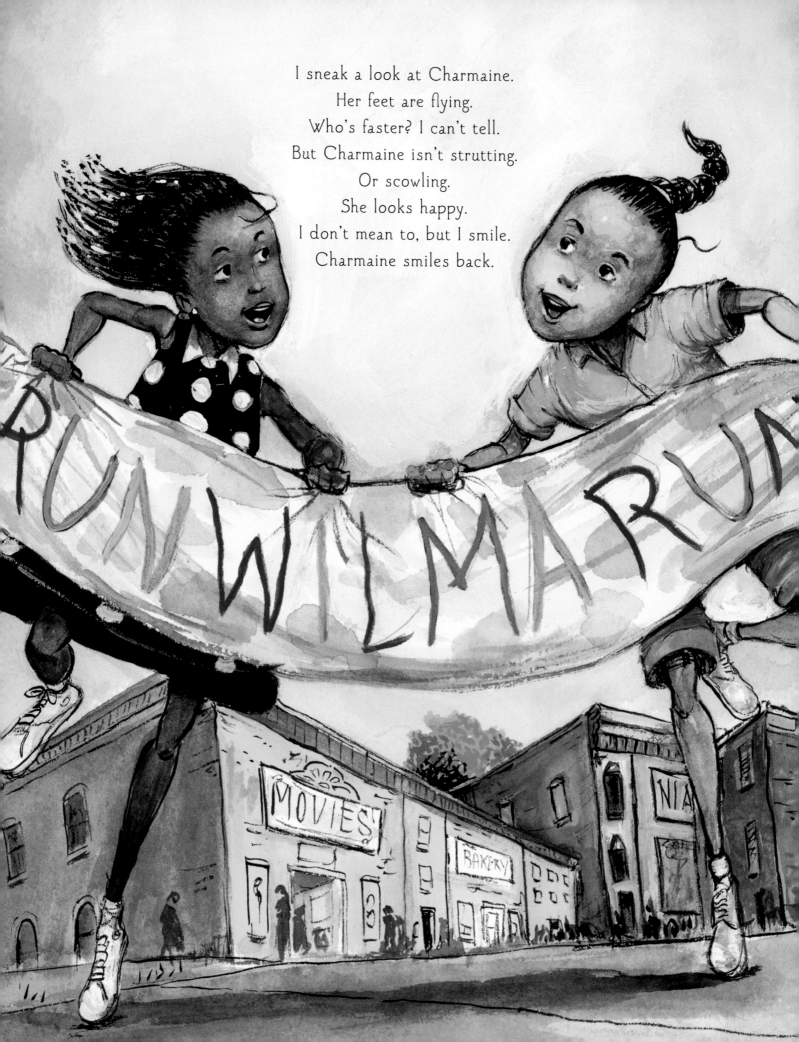

And all at once, I know. Shoes don't matter.
Not as long as we've got our feet.

"Look," I say.
"The perfect spot."

We collapse on the curb.
There are flags. Bands. Noise.
Black faces. And white ones.

And finally, a fancy convertible with the top down.
Right there, holding a bunch of roses, is Wilma Rudolph.
We scream and raise our banner. Hearts pounding. Heads hoping.

Wilma sees us and smiles.
Then she waves.

That makes Charmaine and me
sashay like we own the sidewalk and
everything on it. And maybe—just
maybe—we do.

Because we're the quickest kids
in Clarksville, Tennessee.

And everyone around here knows it.

·······AUTHOR'S NOTE·······

In 1960, African American sprinter Wilma Rudolph was the fastest woman in the world. At the Summer Olympic Games in Rome, Italy, she became the first woman from the United States to win three gold medals at the same Olympics.

Her wins in the 100 meters, 200 meters, and 4x100 relay (with Martha Hudson, Lucinda Williams, and Barbara Jones) made her a household name. She met President John F. Kennedy and received awards including:

- The Associated Press Female Athlete of the Year (in 1960 and 1961).

- The James E. Sullivan Award, which honors character, leadership, and sportsmanship.

- Induction into the U.S. National Track and Field Hall of Fame and the U.S. Olympic Hall of Fame.

George Silk/The LIFE Picture Collection/Getty Images

Wilma's success was even more impressive because of the difficulties she overcame growing up. She was one of twenty-two children, and her family did not have much money. Wilma was often ill as a child and wore a leg brace after she was diagnosed with polio. Doctors didn't think she would ever walk without it, but she exercised and worked for years until her leg was strong.

Wilma grew up in Clarksville, Tennessee, a segregated town. There were separate schools and doctors and restaurants for black people and white people.

After Wilma's victories, Clarksville wanted to honor her with a parade and banquet. Wilma said she would not attend unless the events were integrated—open to everyone. The organizers agreed, and Wilma's celebrations were the first major events for blacks and whites in Clarksville history.

To Mark: Who believed it was possible from the very start.

–P.Z.M.

To my daughter Tiffany, the fastest 4-year-old that I know. Run after your dreams. They are worth the race.

–F.M.

Text copyright © 2016 by Pat Zietlow Miller.
Illustrations copyright © 2016 by Frank Morrison.

Library of Congress Cataloging-in-Publication Data:

Miller, Pat Zietlow, author.
   The quickest kid in Clarksville / by Pat Zietlow Miller ; illustrations by Frank Morrison.
        pages cm
   Summary: Growing up in the segregated town of Clarksville, Tennessee, in the 1960s, Alta's family cannot afford to buy her new sneakers–but she still plans to attend the parade celebrating her hero Wilma Rudolph's three Olympic gold medals.
   ISBN 978-1-4521-2936-5 (alk. paper)
   1. Rudolph, Wilma–Juvenile fiction. 2. African American girls–Tennessee–Clarksville–Juvenile fiction. 3. Role models–Juvenile fiction. 4. Parades–Tennessee–Clarksville–Juvenile fiction. 5. Segregation–Tennessee–Clarksville–Juvenile fiction. 6. Clarksville (Tenn.)–History–20th century–Juvenile fiction. [1. Rudolph, Wilma–Fiction. 2. African Americans–Fiction. 3. Role models–Fiction. 4. Parades–Fiction. 5. Segregation–Fiction. 6. Running–Fiction. 7. Clarksville (Tenn.)–History–20th century–Fiction.] I. Morrison, Frank, 1971- illustrator. II. Title.
   PZ7.M63224Qu 2016
   813.6–dc23
   2014018358

Manufactured in China.

Design by Ryan Hayes.
Typeset in Aged and Harman.
The illustrations in this book were rendered in watercolor.

10 9 8 7 6 5 4 3 2 1

Chronicle Books LLC
680 Second Street
San Francisco, California 94107

Chronicle Books–we see things differently. Become part of our community at www.chroniclekids.com.